I0734469

THE BILLIONAIRE'S DAUGHTER

A Davidson And Harper Mystery

MICHAEL KINGSWOOD

Copyright © 2012 by Michael Kingswood

Cover Art Copyright © Nikolay Okhitin | Dreamstime.com
and Elena Titarenco | Dreamstime.com

ISBN 13: 978-1-950683-24-6

ISBN 10: 1-950683-24-9

This story is a work of fiction. Names, characters, places, and incidents are either products of the author's imagination or used fictitiously. Any resemblance to actual events, locales, or persons, living or dead, is entirely coincidental.

All rights reserved.

No part of this book may be reproduced in any form or by any electronic or mechanical means, including information storage and retrieval systems, without written permission from the author, except for the use of brief quotations in a book review.

Parties interested in licensing rights to this property, should contact publisher@ssnstorytelling.com.

Contents

About This Book

The strong-willed daughter of a wealthy man. The son of a notorious mob boss. And his grandmother's engagement ring.

Just another day on the job for private investigators Ronald Harper and Kathleen Davidson.

The Billionaire's Daughter is a 5,900 word short mystery.

Enjoy the book! After you're done, please come to Michael's website and sign up for his mailing list at michaelkingswood.com/newsletter-signup/. Guaranteed to be spam free, he uses it to announce new releases and special promotions for his fans.

The Billionaire's Daughter

Ronald checked his piece, tucked into a holster in the small of his back, then drew a deep breath and opened the door.

Warm light, muted music, and pleasant odors greeted him as he stepped inside. La Mer had a reputation as one of the best restaurants in town, and from the entryway alone, it looked to live up to it. Ronald felt underdressed in his khaki pants and leather jacket over a green collared shirt. Everyone else was in suits and evening gowns, or tuxedos.

The maitre d', a rotund man of around fifty who wore a formal tuxedo and presided over his domain from behind a mahogany lectern with the restaurant's logo engraved in the front, looked him up and down in disapproval. "Welcome to La Mer," he said in a lofty, I'm-better-than-you-and-we-both-know-it tone.

"Hello," Ronald said. "I'm meeting someone for dinner at seven thirty."

The maitre d's eyes flicked to the clock on the wall, and he frowned. "It is now seven forty-five, sir."

"I like to be fashionably late." Ronald winked at him.

"We have a strict dress code, sir. Sport coats and ties, no exception."

"Well, I'm sure that..."

"No exception!"

Shit. Now what? Ronald thought about trying to bribe his way in, but quickly dismissed that idea. This was the kind of place where they would call the cops on you for something like that.

"We do have coats and ties you may rent for the evening, if you wish," said the maitre d'.

"You do?"

The other man shrugged. "It is not an extensive collection, but you may find something that will fit." He gestured off to the left, where a homely young lady in a white collared shirt and black pants manned the restaurant's coat closet. Ronald could see a number of overcoats on the racks there, but few blazers. Oh well, never know til you try.

"Thanks," he said and turned away.

"Certainly, sir," came the pompous reply from astern.

Ronald was in luck. They had one coat in his size, 46 Regular. And wonder of wonders, it was not completely hideous. The tie was another matter entirely; it clashed with both his shirt and the coat. Beggars can't be choosers though, so he accepted both and soon enough he was dressed "appropriately", though quite a bit lighter in the wallet. The rental fee was outrageous.

He walked past the maitre d' and into the restaurant proper, trying hard to keep his normal swagger.

La Mer's layout was fairly typical: a bar manned by a pair of white-shirted bartenders at the front, with the dining area further back. It was the design of the place that set it apart. The bar was topped in marble and a quick glance showed only top-shelf liquors in their selection. The dining area reeked of opulence beneath the sumptuous odors of the varied dishes laid out for the customers' consumption. The walls were carved into faux-columns at regular intervals, with numerous paintings that Ronald was sure cost more than his monthly paycheck hanging between them. The furnishing was simple, but carried those little touches of detail that screamed quality if you knew what you were looking at.

It was definitely not his kind of place.

Many eyes followed him as he weaved through the tables. He tried to tell himself it was on account of his dashing good looks and not because he looked ridiculous in his new coat and tie. Himself was hearing none of it, though.

Fortunately, he did not have far to go. He spied Kathleen at a table near the windows, about a third of the way back. She, of course, was dressed to kill in a blue evening gown that matched her eyes, along with a diamond necklace and earrings. She watched him coming with a highly amused expression on her face.

"Good evening," he said as he came to a stop next to her table. "Mind if I join you?"

"I'm not sure I'm worthy to be in the presence of so striking a man."

Ronald rolled his eyes. He sat down across the table from her but stopped for a moment in surprise. "Damn, this is the most comfortable restaurant chair I've ever sat in," he said.

Kathleen quirked an eyebrow upward and shook her head at him. "This *is* La Mer."

"Yeah." Ronald scowled at a prissy little fellow in a tuxedo at the next table over who was staring at him in revulsion. The little guy flinched and looked away quickly. "You could have warned me about the dress code."

Kathleen sniffed. "I assumed you would have the sense to look into it yourself," she replied. "But apparently not."

"Whatever."

The waiter, also dressed in a white collared shirt and black pants - Ronald was beginning to detect a trend - appeared next to the table then with an empty wine glass, which he filled from the bottle already on the table. Opus One, very nice. Whoever the client was, he must have deep pockets.

"Would you like to hear the specials, sir?"

Kathleen made a dismissive little wave with her hand. "No, please," she said before Ronald could speak. The waiter bowed slightly from the waist and departed.

"I actually wanted to hear them."

She sniffed again. "The hell you did. You're going to order a steak, medium, with garlic mashed potatoes and broccoli. Just like always."

Ronald nodded, conceding the point, then lifted his wine glass. "To us," he said.

She smirked, but lifted her glass in turn. The glasses rang like a pair of little bells as they met for the toast. They spare no expense at La Mer, it seemed. No big surprise. He took a long drink from his glass, savoring the exquisite flavor for a moment before swallowing.

"So," he said, turning his head to survey the crowd. "Who's the mark?"

"See the older gentleman..."

"Which one? It's like a geriatric convention in here."

Kathleen was silent for a long moment. Ronald could feel the irritation, and the disapproval, in her stare though he did not look back at her. Finally, she started over.

"Table for six, third from the back along the far wall."

Ronald found it easily. Two men in tuxedos, one in his sixties and the other maybe twenty-five at most, sat in the company of four young ladies in evening gowns. Three of the ladies were a bit plump for his taste, but the last was a hot little brunette number in a green dress, who could have been taken straight from the pages of Playboy. Ronald did a doubletake to make sure he was seeing clearly.

"Who the hell are *they*?"

"They," Katheleen said, "are Marcus Romero and his children."

Wow. That guy had some great genetics, apparently. Wait a minute.

"Marcus Romero the oil tycoon?"

Kathleen nodded.

Ronald whistled softly. Romero was high up on the Forbes 500. If he was the target...

"He's a pretty heavy hitter, Kat. Are you sure about this?"

"It's a job like any other. You're not scared, are you?"

Damn right he was scared. Some people you did *not* mess with. Not without some serious backing. Of course, he was not about to admit that to Kathleen. At least, not yet.

"What's the job?"

She held up one finger and pursed her lips slightly. A few seconds later, the waiter returned and inquired about their order. Ronald ordered his usual, evoking an amused grin from Kathleen, who ordered seared Ahi with mashed potatoes and a side salad. The waiter bowed again and left.

"Apparently," Kathleen said after taking another sip of wine, "Romero's youngest daughter, Isabel, was recently engaged to be married. She called it off but refused to give back the engagement ring."

Ronald looked at her incredulously. "You're kidding."

Kathleen shook her head.

"So our job is to recover a stupid engagement ring from a billionaire's daughter? Christ just buy another one." Seriously, at the rates he and Kathleen charged, that would be far cheaper.

"It's not just any engagement ring. It's a family heirloom of some substantial value."

"Ok, so hire a lawyer. Why us?"

"The former fiancee is...connected." She put special emphasis on the word connected. What was...Aw shit.

Ronald groaned. "Really? She was engaged to a mobster?"

"That is the reason she broke it off. But apparently this particular mobster used his grandmother's engagement ring for the proposal, and didn't tell his father about it beforehand. So..."

"If he makes a big legal stink about it, daddy finds out and maybe he sends some boys over to break her kneecaps to get it back."

Kathleen nods. "He still loves her he says, and doesn't want to see anything bad happen to her. But he *needs* the ring back." She spread her hands and smiled cheerfully. "And so, here we are."

"They must not have been engaged very long, if Daddy didn't meet her and see the ring."

Kathleen shook her head. "About six months."

That didn't make any sense. "Then how..."

"Daddy is Johnny Palmieri."

"Ah." Palmieri was doing five years for racketeering. His son Mario was supposedly running things while Johnny was in the can, but everyone knew Johnny still got regular reports and called a lot of the shots. Ronald looked back at Romero's table and took another drink of wine. "Which one is Isabel?"

"In green."

Ronald grinned. "Lord, I was hoping you were going to say that."

Kathleen rolled her eyes, but Ronald could tell it was from amusement more than disapproval.

There was not much else to say about it, so Ronald took another drink and leaned back in his chair. Might as well enjoy dinner. Lord knew when he would ever have the chance to eat at La Mer again.

Dinner was exquisite, exceeding his every expectation. The meat was perfectly prepared and seasoned, and seemed to melt in his mouth, it was so tender. It was hard to keep an eye on the Romero table with such a feast in front of him. But he was a professional, so he managed.

They finished eating several minutes before Kathleen and he did, but made no move to get up. Perhaps they had ordered desert, or were meeting friends? Regardless, their finishing was a sign for him and Kathleen to go. The trick was to finish and go without appearing to rush, which would have drawn attention.

Kathleen handled the check, then they were off. Five minutes later, they sat in Ronald's car in the parking lot, watching the entrance through a couple of small binoculars Ronald kept under his car seat.

"She has her own place, right?"

"She's twenty-four years old. I certainly hope she does," Kathleen replied.

"You never know with these rich girls... Ok, there she is."

Isabel's dress was easy to spot. She came out after the rest of her family and hung back from them while they waited for the valets to retrieve their vehicles.

"How long ago did she break it off with mob-boy?"

"About a month ago."

"Hmm. Looks like the rest of the family may be giving her the cold shoulder over it."

Beside him, Kathleen snickered.

One by one, the Romeros got in their cars and drove away, until only Marcus himself and Isabel remained. Through the binoculars, they appeared to be talking heatedly about something. Isabel was wagging a finger in his face; she was pissed! Then a blue Boxter pulled up and a valet got out. Isabel snatched the key out of the valet's hand and got in, then sped off out of the parking lot and down the street. Marcus slumped, clearly upset or resigned about whatever had just transpired, and turned away.

"Poor guy," Ronald mused.

"Yeah, I'm crying a river for him. Get after her!"

Ronald grinned at Kathleen. Leave it to her to suppress empathy beneath professionalism. But she was right. He started up the engine and pulled out onto the street.

The Boxter was already a block ahead of them, and moving at a high rate of speed. There was no way Ronald could overtake Isabel in his Outback. But then, he did not have to. As long as he kept her in sight, it was all good.

But that was easier said than done. Isabel veered around corners at breakneck speed and zoomed in and out of traffic like a madwoman. She must really have been pissed off. Or at least, Ronald hoped that was why she was driving like that. Otherwise, she was a highway fatality waiting to happen.

He lost sight of her for a panicked minute as she zoomed around two turns in quick succession. Only Kathleen looking down a side-street and spotting her saved the night. Eventually, she slowed down as she got into the more opulent area of town. Single family houses gave way to mansions, and she assumed a more stately pace. Don't want to piss off the neighbors, after all.

Finally, she pulled into a circular driveway in front of a large but not over-the-top house backing up to a small lake, probably man-made. Ronald pulled to a stop a few houses...mansions...away, made a note of the address, and broke out the binoculars again.

Isabel stormed into the house, leaving the front door wide open. She remained out of sight for almost fifteen minutes. When she came back out, Ronald almost did not recognize her. She wore cut-off blue jeans and a white t-shirt with a logo or design of some sort on the front. Her hair was pulled back in a ponytail and she had discarded most of her jewelry.

"She could almost pass for a real person," Kathleen observed from the seat beside Ronald.

He laughed.

Isabel got back into the Boxter and pulled out of the driveway, then turned left and drove back toward downtown.

Thirty minutes later, Ronald led Kathleen into a dimly-lit nightclub. Bearing the super-original name The Techno, the place was much like every other nightclub Ronald had ever been in, if perhaps a bit on the seedy side. The same annoying "dance" music thumped over the speakers as in every other place, loud enough to make conversation difficult in anything less than a shout. The bar was battered, with scratches in the counter and stickers of various sorts posted all over. It held a standard low-brow booze selection and sat in the predictable location over on the right. The dance floor was in back beneath multi-colored spotlights, with the DJ station on a raised platform off to the left above the floor. The place smelled of booze and sweat, and the floor was sticky in spots from spilled drinks, and possibly other fluids Ronald did not want to think about.

Overall, not a very inspiring location, and not the sort of place Ronald would have expected a spoiled little rich girl to frequent. Kathleen was over-dressed for it. But not by much. Many of the women there were dressed up in club attire. Still, Ronald noticed a few people eyeing her askance. Best not to keep her here for long. He got the impression this was not always the safest place.

Isabel seemed to like it, though. Ronald spotted her after a minute's looking, shaking it up on the dance floor with abandon. Men and women danced around her, but she did not appear to be with any of them. Ronald continued to watch her as he and Kathleen meandered over to the bar, and she gave no less than three guys the brush-off.

"Ok, now what?"

Ronald looked at Kathleen and grinned. "I'll keep her busy here. You go search her place." He held out the keys to his car.

Kathleen looked incredulously at him. "You're going to keep her busy."

"Yup."

She snorted. "Now this I have to see."

Ronald shook his head. "No, now you need to get out of here." He leaned closer. "You're a bit over-dressed."

Kathleen scowled, but she nodded. She was a professional, after all. "Alright." She snatched the keys from Ronald's hand. "Text me when she's on her way home. I don't want to be there when she gets back."

Ronald nodded and gave her a little salute, then he turned and headed out to the dance floor.

Some men have trouble meeting women in clubs. Ronald was not one of them. He had no idea why. Maybe it was the fact that he actually knew how to dance; several years of ballroom training back in Junior High and High School still paid dividends. Maybe it was because he acted like a gentlemen. Or maybe it was just his jacket. Either way, after a few minutes dancing around, he maneuvered closer to Isabel, and sure enough, she flashed him a smile.

Sometimes it was just too easy.

They danced together for five songs before she stepped off the dance floor, gesturing toward the bar. Ronald followed. She ordered a scotch and soda. Ronald mulled it over and went with a seven and seven, earning a look of amusement from her.

"What?" he asked, "You don't like Seven-Up?"

Isabel shrugged. "From the way you dance, I figured you for something a bit stronger."

Ronald wasn't sure how to take that, to be honest. It was not often he found himself without a pithy comeback, but just then he had nothing.

"Well, I like a seven and seven sometimes."

Isabel laughed and ran her hand down his arm. "Don't be grumpy. I didn't mean anything."

"It would be easier to take if I knew your name. I'm Ron."

"Isabel."

They shook hands, and the bartender brought back their drinks. Ron reached for his wallet, but Isabel placed her hand over his, preventing him from taking it out of his pocket.

"I've got this one," she said. "Payback for the dances."

"Far be it from me to pass up a drink from a lovely lady."

Isabel laughed again. It was a good sign when he made a woman laugh. Well, usually. He was not joking though. She was great-looking in the restaurant, and from afar. Up close, she was stunning. And that was dressed-down. He could understand mob-boy's affection, though he was surprised a guy like that would so readily let a girl like her go.

They sipped their drinks and exchanged small talk for a while. Or as best they could with all the music blaring in their ears anyway. She worked as a commodities trader in the local exchange. Liked running and was training for a triathlon. Had a dog once, but after he died could never bring herself to get another one. Enjoyed travel; Prague was her favorite foreign city. Spoke Spanish and German. She never mentioned her billionaire father, though; smart of her.

Ronald answered questions about himself as they came, but for the most part let her do the talking. He had found that people enjoyed talking about themselves, and would happily do so with just a bit of prodding. It made his line of work a whole lot easier, that was for sure. All at once, though, she stopped talking and looked over his shoulder at something. Then her eyes widened slightly and she slouched down against the bar, pushing closer to him. She was using him as concealment from someone in the rear of the club, Ronald realized quickly.

"What's wrong?"

Isabel replied in a strained voice, "Those three guys are friends of my ex. Shit, they never come here!"

Ronald looked over his shoulder and instantly saw who she was talking about. Three guys, not particularly big but obviously muscular, dressed sharply but in the sort of way that screams ,"Gumbah". They stood near the door, surveying the scene like hunters seeking out prey.

"Have they been giving you problems?" Ronald looked back at her. He would lose track of what they were doing by looking away, but it would be worse to make eye contact; it would just draw attention to himself, and her. Moving casually, he repositioned himself slightly, to afford her better cover as well.

Isabel nodded, keeping her head down.

"All right. Let's get out of here." Ronald took hold of Isabel's arm gently. "Follow me and do exactly what I say, ok?"

She looked up at him. There was fear in her eyes, but also confusion laced with curiosity. Who was this guy who was suddenly trying to play the hero? Ronald could practically hear the thought streaming through her head.

"I have a bit of experience with these sorts of situations. Will you trust me?"

She hesitated, then nodded.

"Ok. Get your car keys out."

Ronald glanced back at the Gumbahs. They had moved away from the exit and were making their way toward the dance floor, spread out so they could cover more area. The closest one would be in a position to see Isabel in a few seconds.

"When I say, run to the exit as fast as you can. I'll be right behind you."

The Gumbah was close. It was now or never.

"Get ready," Ronald said, then he turned and, moving in a lurch as though he was drunk, stumbled headlong into the Gumbah.

"Get off me, motherfucker!" The Gumbah shoved him. Hard.

Ronald stumbled backward a step, then threw up his hands and said, "Hey man, I'm sorry man," making sure to slur his words. The Gumbah looked at him in disgust. Then the thug's eyes widened as he recognized Isabel behind Ronald. He stepped forward, toward her.

"Go!" As he shouted, Ronald kicked as hard as he could. His foot connected with the side of the Gumbah's knee. He could not hear the sound of bone or ligaments snapping over the roar of the speakers, but from the way the thug dropped instantly, grabbing at his knee and rolling with an agonized expression on his face, Ronald knew he had caused some major damage.

He did not wait to see if the other two had noticed or not. He turned and raced toward the entrance. Isabel was already out the door; she could be quick when she needed to, it seemed.

Ronald brushed past the bouncer at the door and scurried up the stairs to street level, shoving past individuals and one small group who were on their way down and earning chagrined curses from one and all. Better than getting shot in the back. Bursting through the door, he stumbled to a stop outside and looked around.

The parking lot stood, about two thirds full, across the street from the club's building. Clubbers, dressed for the party and laughing up a storm, congregated around cars, either just arriving or getting ready to leave. The street stretched left and right for several blocks before turning, with darkened buildings at intervals on either side.

Isabel was nowhere to be seen. Shit.

Frantically looking left and right, he saw movement in the alley entrance next the building. She could not be that stupid, could she? He darted toward the alley and just got around the corner enough to make out a white shirt, jeans, and a female's shape when something slammed into his cheek from the side. Hard.

He went down in a heap, his head ringing and his cheek already beginning to swell painfully. Then a boot struck him in the gut, sending him rolling over into a couple of trash cans, upending one of them and sending refuse spilling out all around him. He lay there, stunned, tasting his own blood from where he bit his lip in the impact and trying not to absorb the stink of the spilled trash.

Isabel let out a panicked shout and ran. He could hear the sound of her light footfalls receding into the alley. Larger, heavier footsteps followed. At least they didn't stay to beat on him.

Sudden fury, at himself and at the situation, flared within Ronald, and he forced himself to roll back over onto his belly and place his hands beneath himself. He had to stop there for a few seconds while the world stopped spinning. Then he took a deep breath and pushed himself up onto his hands and knees. It felt like he was lifting the world, but it worked.

He raised his head. The alley contained no streetlights, but he could make out some details from the lights in the parking lots across the street. Two bulky forms stood near the wall about halfway down the alley. One of them was pushing a smaller body, Isabel he was certain, up against the wall by her throat. Ronald heard a deep voice saying something, but the thug was talking low enough that he could not make out the words.

Ronald took another deep breath. Time for that hero bit. Why did it always have to be the hero bit?

He forced himself up to his feet, using the trash can for support along the way, and stood swaying for as long as he dared. Which was not long, with Isabel alone with those two. He checked his holster - yep still there - and drew his Glock, then moved down the alley toward Isabel and the Gumbahs as quickly as he could.

"...wants it back."

"Fuck you, Marty. It's mine." Ronald had to give it to her, Isabel was tough. Maybe not the smartest ever, but tough.

Marty, the Gumbah doing the talking, drew back as though to hit her.

"That's about enough of that, Marty," Ronald said, drawing a bead on him over the sights of his Glock.

The Gumbahs both turned their heads in surprised anger that quickly gave way to nervous wariness when they saw Ronald's gun. For a second, everyone stood perfectly still, the thugs clearly considering whether he was willing to shoot and Isabel looking at him with a mixture of surprise, gratitude, and hope.

"Alright Marty, have your pal let her go, then both of you put your hands up and back away, nice and slow."

Ronald learned the tone of voice that makes people obey without question in the Marines Corps. It worked just as well on these Gumbahs as it had on wet-behind-the-ears privates from flyover country. They released Isabel and backed up as commanded, but scowled darkly at him.

"You're digging your own grave, you know that, motherfucker?" Marty said.

Ronald shrugged. "Maybe." Glancing aside at Isabel, he said, "Still got your keys?"

She nodded, her eyes still wide with fright. She was trembling visibly.

"Go get your car and pull it to the front of the alley."

She nodded again. Pausing only to say, "Thank you," in a voice that trembled as much as her arms and legs did, she hurried away.

Once she was out of earshot, it was time to talk business. "Johnny Palmieri sent you guys to get the ring back, huh?"

Marty blinked, surprise flashing across his features, then he nodded.

"Thought so. Look, you tell him his son will have the ring back to him by the end of the week, ok? Until then, leave the girl alone."

Marty just scowled. That was probably the best Ronald was going to get, so he began slowly backing away from them, toward the mouth of the alley. He was almost there when, with a screeching of tires, the Boxter came to a halt and its passenger door popped open. He breathed a sigh of relief; he had not been entirely sure she was going to come back for him.

"Tell your buddy sorry about his knee," he called out to the Gumbahs, then he leapt into the car and slammed the door shut. "Drive. Fast."

In retrospect, the last part of the order was neither required nor desired. Isabel floored it, and the Boxter surged ahead with more acceleration than he had ever experienced in a car before. Goddamn, this ride was sweet. Ronald twisted around in his seat and saw the thugs rush out of the alley behind them, but they did not pursue, at least not immediately.

"Looks like we're in the clear," he reported.

Isabel nodded, her eyes flickering from the rearview mirror to him and then back to the street ahead. "Are you a cop?"

Ronald shook his head and slid his hips forward on the seat so he could re-holster his Glock. "I'm a Private Investigator."

She blinked, then shook her head and laughed, sounding almost like the girl he had talked to at the bar again. "You're kidding. Like in the movies?"

"Something like that. Look," Ronald fixed her with the most serious look he knew how to give. "You really need to give Mario Palmieri his grandmother's ring back."

Isabel's eyes widened and she slammed on the brakes. The car fishtailed briefly as it slowed then came to a halt, and Ronald had to press his palms against the dashboard to avoid being thrown into the windshield.

"Are you fucking kidding me? You too? You need to get the fuck out of this car, right now!"

"Isabel, listen to me..."

"GET OUT!"

Ronald did not reach for the door handle. "Mario gave that ring to you without..."

She made as if to slap him, but Ronald caught her hand in mid-swing and held it still in a firm grip at the wrist.

"He gave it to you without his father's permission. He hired me and my partner to get it back from you because he didn't want his father finding out and doing something bad to you." She tried to pull back, but he tightened his grip on her wrist. She winced, but made no sound. "It looks like he found out anyway; that's why Marty and his buddies were after you tonight. The only way out of this is to give it back."

It's also the required thing to do when you dump a guy after you've agreed to marry him, Ronald did not say.

Isabel was silent for a full minute, scowling at him the whole time. Then, finally, she blew his mind.

"So that whole bit on the dance floor and at the bar was bullshit?" Were their tears in her eyes? "Dammit, I *liked* you."

Ronald could not remember when he had been so surprised. He released Isabel's wrist and dropped his hand into his lap, unsure what to say for a moment. Ah fuck it, just be straight up. "Not completely. Yes, I was there for the job. But I like you also. And I *sure* don't want to see anything bad happen to you."

Isabel stared at him, saying nothing. Ronald began to wonder if she was going to get out of the car herself or something silly like that. But then she sighed and nodded.

"It's an ugly ring, anyway."

She put the car into gear and sped off down the road again.

Ronald laughed in spite of himself. "Then why the hell did you not give it back to begin with?"

"Principle."

"Come again?"

Isabel glanced at him, looking a trifle annoyed. "Principle. He lied to me the whole time we were together. He makes his living by hurting other people." She took a deep breath, then said in a somewhat petulant tone, "I just thought he should suffer a little bit himself."

Ronald was forced to admit, there was a certain

logic and poetic justice about that train of thought. Pity they lived in the real world, where trying that sort of thing is likely to get a person hurt or killed. But still a halfway decent thought.

"Where do you keep it?"

"In a safe at work where we keep our client information. Very secure."

"Alright. Let's go."

Isabel shook her head. "It's a double-combination safe, and I only have one of them." Her lips turned up into a sly grin and she raised an eyebrow at him. "Very secure."

She was not kidding. Ronald had seen a couple safes like that in the Corps, but they were only used for highly classified stuff like crypto. Her firm took protection of their customer information seriously. He made a mental note to look into the requirements to open an account there. Later.

"Ok. Then first thing in the morning, get it and bring it by my office." He reached into the inner pocket of his leather jacket and pulled out a business card, which he laid on the center console.

Isabel pursed her lips. "How do I know you'll get it to Mario? Maybe I should just bring it to him myself."

That would make it hard for me to get paid, Ronald didn't say. "Remember, his father's goon's are looking for you. That could get pretty ugly. And besides," he looked quizzically at her, "do you *really* want to see Mario again? He's just going to beg you to come back to him, you know."

Isabel considered that and nodded. "You've got a point. Alright, your office at ten o'clock?"

"Sure."

"It's a date." She flashed him a quick smile that made a little shiver of excitement run down

Ronald's spine. She was a little minx, wasn't she? "So where should I drop you off?"

Ronald was half-tempted to suggest her place, just to see what could happen. But his wiser head prevailed and he gestured toward the card. "My office will be fine."

Isabel nodded silently. Was that disappointment that he saw in her eyes for a second? Surely not.

He settled back into the sculpted car seat, and they drove in silence the rest of the way to his building. He and Kathleen rented a small office on the second floor of a little commercial building downtown. A drug store and a falafel joint dominated the sign space out front, so it was very easy to miss the little sign that read "Davidson and Harper, Private Investigators" next to a narrow glass door at the end of the building.

Isabel pulled to a stop and looked his building over for a moment. "Well, here we are."

"Yep." Ronald opened the car door. "See you at ten."

"I'll be there," she smiled. Then she leaned over and gave him a light kiss on the cheek. The brush of her lips sent another rush of excitement through him. "Thanks again for helping me with those guys," she said as she pulled back from the kiss, her breath hot against his cheek.

Ronald swallowed hard and put on his best nonchalant smile. Or at least he hoped it was nonchalant. "My pleasure," he said. Their eyes met, and he felt drawn into hers. He had not noticed the flecks of yellow buried in the green of her irises before. She really did have nice...

He broke that chain of thought and looked away, clearing his throat. "Until tomorrow then," he said, somewhat lamely. Then he got out of the car and closed the door. He thought he saw her smile in amusement for a moment before she pulled away.

It was only when he was unable to open that little glass door leading up to his office that he remembered he did not have his keys. And that he had not texted Kathleen yet.

She was going to be pissed.

Message From The Author

Thank you for reading my book. I hope you enjoyed reading it as much as I enjoyed writing it.

Every review helps an author out, so whether you loved this book, hated it, or something in between, please take a minute to tell other readers what you thought. All of the online retailers make it very easy to do, and I would really appreciate it.

Feel free to come say hi at my website or on Facebook. I always enjoy hearing from readers, especially since you all are, collectively, my boss.

I also have a weekly podcast, Story Time With Michael Kingswood, where I read stories and talk through some of the latest goings on in my world. I'd love to see you there.

Thanks again. My best to you and yours.

Warm Regards,
Michael Kingswood

Mailing List

If you enjoyed this book and would like word on new releases and special deals from Michael Kingswood, sign up for his newsletter on his website. Guaranteed to be spam-free, you can opt out at any time. And you can rest assured he will not share your information with anyone, for any reason.

https://michaelkingswood.com/newsletter-signup/

Supporting Patronage

Michael would like to invite you to become a supporting member of his website. Similar in concept to Patreon, a few dollars a month will give you access to exclusive content, and help him to focus more of his time to writing fun and exciting stories for your enjoyment.

Sign up at his website:

https://www.michaelkingswood.com/
membership/supporting-patronage/

About The Author

Michael Kingswood is 20-year veteran of the US Navy submarine force and a lifelong fan of science fiction and fantasy literature. His work has appeared in numerous collections and anthologies, to include the Fiction River Anthology series from WMG publishing. He holds a bachelors degree in Mechanical Engineering as well as a Master of Engineering Management and a Master of Business Administration. He has four children and currently resides in San Diego.

Find Michael Kingswood online at:

www.michaelkingswood.com

www.facebook.com/michael.kingswood

steemit.com/@michaelkingswood

More Books By Michael Kingswood

Glimmer Vale Chronicles

Glimmer Vale

Out-Dweller

Tollard's Peak

Robbed Blind

Wedding Gifts: A Glimmer Vale Chronicles Story

The Falconer's Stairs

Glimmer Vale Omnibus Edition #1

The Pericles Conspiracy

Passing In The Night

The Pericles Conspiracy

Dawn Of Enlightenment

Masters Of The Sun

Novellas

What Lurks Between

The Necromancer's Lair

The Champion

Veritas Morte

Story Collections

Tales Of Adventure #1

Tales Of Adventure #2

Short Story 10-Pack

A Jar Of Mixed Treats

Short Fiction

Michael has also published a number of shorter works,
links to which can be found on his website.

Copyright © 2012 Michael Kingswood

Cover Art Copyright © Nikolay Okhitin | Dreamstime.com
and Elena Titarenco | Dreamstime.com

This story is a work of fiction. Names, characters, places, and
incidents are either products of the author's imagination or
used fictitiously. Any resemblance to actual events, locales, or
persons, living or dead, is entirely coincidental.

All rights reserved.

No part of this book may be reproduced in any form or by any
electronic or mechanical means, including information storage
and retrieval systems, without written permission from the
author, except for the use of brief quotations in a book review.

Parties interested in licensing rights to this property, should
contact publisher@ssnstorytelling.com.

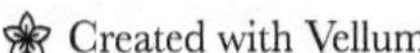 Created with Vellum

www.ingramcontent.com/pod-product-compliance
Lightning Source LLC
Chambersburg PA
CBHW032053180726

48284CB00004B/1326